The Brimstone Journals

The Brimstone Journals

Ron Koertge

CANDLEWICK PRESS
CAMBRIDGE, MASSACHUSETTS

Thanks to my friends on the faculty of the MFA in
Writing for Children program at Vermont College.
Also to Robin Behn and to Jan Uebersetzig.

First edition 2001

Library of Congress Cataloging-in-Publication Data

Koertge, Ronald.
The Brimstone journals / Ron Koertge. — 1st ed.
p.   cm.
Summary: In a series of short interconnected poems, students
at a high school nicknamed Brimstone reveal the violence
existing and growing in their lives.
ISBN 0-7636-1302-9
1. High school students — Poetry. 2. Violence in adolescence —
Poetry. 3. School violence — Poetry. [1. Violence — Poetry.
2. High schools — Poetry. 3. Schools — Poetry.] I. Title.
PS3561.O347 B7 2001
811'.54 — dc21   00-037886

2 4 6 8 10 9 7 5 3 1

Printed in the United States of America

This book was typeset in Caecilia.

Candlewick Press
2067 Massachusetts Avenue
Cambridge, Massachusetts 02140

For Bianca

meredith

Jennifer

joseph

TRAN

Lester

Sheila

Allison

Kelli

DAMON

ROB

CARTER

neesha

david

Boyd

kitty

I

Lester

My dad'd freak if he knew I played
with it, but I can't help myself. And
I'm not hurting anybody.

The bullets are across the room
in his sock drawer. The Glock is by
the bed, same place as the condoms.

I like to hold it in my hand. Everything
gets sharper, I don't know why.

I feel skinnier instead of just this big
bag of fries and Coke and pepperoni.

If I take off my clothes, it's cool
on my skin.

I'd never hurt anybody but if I did
this is how I'd do it — butt naked.

And I'd start in the gym. They wouldn't
laugh then, would they? The jocks would
crap their pants. The girls'd kiss my fat
feet.

TRAN

My father came here with his parents when
he was ten. In the boat, there was room
for two to sleep, so they took turns
standing up.

By 1980 they owned a small market.
By 1990 three more. My mother and father
often worked twenty hours a day. I started
stocking shelves at age six.

Everybody warned against black people,
but who turned out to be full of hatred
for our prosperity? Others like us, some
from a village not five kilometers away
from where my mother was born.

Father does not want me to forget the country
I have never seen. Every day an hour of
Vietnamese only. Then another of music
with traditional instruments.

He wants me to be richer than he, more
successful. Yet he begrudges one hundred
dollars for the ugly new glasses I need.

His dreams are like a box I cannot put down.

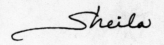

I don't think I deserve to be Monica's
best friend. I mean, I am, but . . .

Sometimes I feel like she adopted me,
like she went to the People Pound
and there I was panting through the
wire door.

I'm not the type that gets chosen,
you know? So why me? But I love
it. I love her.

Sometimes when I sleep over, she
just walks out of her clothes while
she's talking to me. She's got these
little golden hairs on her stomach.

If I'm a lesbian, my dad is going
to kill me!

DAMON

We are the champions!

Numero Uno!!

Half of us already got scholarships,
full ride.

Everybody loves us — chicks, teachers,
everybody!!

Man, standing out there in the center
of the gym in my letterman's jacket
with my buddies. It's the best!

And Kelli. She'll do anything
to stay my girlfriend.

Anything!!!

Kelli♡

Damon is driving me crazy. He's got like
our whole life planned: college, jobs, kids,
even what kind of car he'll buy for me.

Already it's always the same. He picks me
up, we drive around, bump into some of
the kids. If I so much as say hi to another guy
he loses it. Then we argue. Then we park
someplace and do it.

It's like that Bill Murray movie where the same
day keeps happening over and over. Except this
isn't funny.

I was talking to a new kid the other day
who's in my Music Appreciation class. He's
black but not, you know, *black* black.

Cool dresser, kind of like Will Smith. He's
from Washington and he's seen everything I've
seen, except he didn't have to rent it.

We were talking about this movie called
Invaders from Mars where the townies turn
into mutants when they fall into the sand pit
where the aliens landed.

He said he wished his parents would take
a little walk out there and I said I wished
Damon would. Then we both laughed.

When's the last time I did that with a guy?

Boyd

Dad drifts in about three A.M. a couple of nights ago, and I'm just finishing up *Dog Day Afternoon* for the nineteenth time.

He's still a little faded and sometimes that makes him all paternal, so he gets us a couple of beers. I've seen this before when he's shot some pretty good pool and some hootchie's told him he looks like Harrison Ford.

Things are gonna change, he says. There's gonna be a lunch for me to take to school every day, sandwiches with that brown mustard. No more doing his laundry.
And you know that dog I always wanted?
It's mine.

Part of me wants it to be true so bad my teeth hurt. But I'm not holding my breath.

"So how's school?"

Here we go.
After he calls me stupid about ten times,
I split. I run for like a block but I'm totally out of shape, so I just walk until I stop wanting to kill him. Then I crash in the basement.

neesha

I don beleave in the white man sway.
I beleave thoze rools of hiz — dat
spellin, hiz gramma, doze frag mints
and common splizes — I beleave
awl them roolz r jis another way
2 keep my black brotherz and sistahs
down.

Moore house niggah rewards 4 stayin
in da kitchen.

Sew — dat aint 4 me. I reef-use 2
conform, purrform, or reef-orm.

I can do it if I want to, see?
Eye jist doan wan 2.

Lester

I'm out at Wal-Mart with my mom,
loading up the shopping cart. She works
days, Dad nights. All so they can buy more crap.

Man, it reminds me way too much of this
movie on TV where a bunch of slaves
were moving some big statue of a god.

They had it on these logs that were like
rollers and most of the slaves pushed
this god while the rest picked up
the last log and hustled it around to
the front. And they did this all day.

Boyd

School's got a thousand rules. I've
only got one —

> BREAK
> ALL
> RULES.

Do any of those goddamned things
make sense?

Drive carefully? Fuck that. Let the other
guy get out of my way.

Don't smoke? Fuck you. It's my lungs.

Love your neighbor? Well, actually, I
did kind of like my old neighbor 'cause
he had a meth lab in his basement.
The new guy is not so cool. Him and his
big noisy dog. (Not for long, though.)

joseph

Dad played the whale songs tape while Mom
patted down the lentil loaf. Then we had
a long talk about the compost heap.

They're going to ride twenty miles on their
bikes tomorrow to buy one hundred percent
plastic shoes. Do I want to go?

Get serious. The cow is dead, okay? Wear
a pair of cool kicks for a change.

Mom wants to know if anybody has to use
the bathroom. She needs to take a couple
of cleansing enemas because she had
to ride behind a truck today and feels
toxic.

My folks are weird, but at least they have
a good time: they drink a lot of wine, boogie
to the Dead, giggle in the bedroom.

There's this girl at school I kind of like
but her parents are pleasure-impaired:
no drinking, no dancing, no sex. She's
guilty about everything.

What do I feel guilty about? Throwing away
that Diet Coke can.

Allison

A thirty-nine-year-old man in California
drives his Cadillac into a playground
and kills two kids because he wanted
to execute innocent children.

That isn't a sign of social collapse?

Twenty-five million teenagers go to
twenty thousand schools in the U.S.
Ten kids, TEN KIDS, in seven schools
did *all* the shooting, ALL OF IT,
in 1998–99.

In the same two years, grownups
in southern California alone massacred
forty people.

I know what I'm talking about. I did
research for this paper I had to write.
I got a B- because my report "wasn't
focused."

Really? Could that be because when I
was typing it my stepfather kept trying
to massage my shoulders because I looked
"tense"?

I've told him I hate that. I've told my mom.
She says he's just being friendly.

Kelli♡

When I told Damon I was home
but didn't feel like picking up,
he just freaked.

Yelled about how it made him
look when all the other guys knew
where their girlfriends were.

Boyd

I'm down at the ARCO station scraping
dimes out of the glove box to buy three
dollars worth when this black dude
in a Beemer pulls right in front of me
and holds out a fifty.

I couldn't fucking believe it.

The gas jockey (Mike) gives that chucker
his Full fucking Service. Then starts
talking to me about the purity of the white
race. Says sometimes he feels like he's
going to explode.

Man, that is it exactly!

kitty

I see things other people can't.
Like fat.

I know when I'm fat and I'm fat
now.

If I wasn't, I wouldn't have to
wear these big clothes.

Jennifer

Daddy says God talks to us, but our minds
are too busy to hear. Too much TV, radio,
gossip.

He says if I'm ever confused about anything
I should take a calming breath and ask, "What
would Jesus do?"

I try, but nothing happens. Okay, I can't see Him
loaning His homework to slackers, rolling
a doobie, or hiding a handgun in His robe,
but that isn't the same thing as getting an answer.

Daddy says I should testify at school. I can just
picture me telling Meredith I was washed in the
blood of the Lamb. You know what she'd say?
"Is that as hard to get out as grape juice?"

She's a slut, but her complexion is perfect.
You'd think a bad person wouldn't have
such good skin.

Reverend Powell says everything will be revealed
in God's own good time.

I could be a pastor's wife, I think. His hands
in the healing circle are soft. But strong.

Rob

A teacher comes down on me the other day. He's heard stories. Are they true?

I said, "Maybe. Like it's any of your business."

"Well, you should be ashamed. Sex isn't a game."

I'm not about to argue with some guy in a clip-on tie, but just for the record:

If it isn't a game, why does everybody keep score?

meredith

I'm eighteen, can look twenty-one
easy. I like guys. And guys like me.

Rob and his crew think they're such
studs. They're kids.

I like somebody who'll take me
someplace really nice. Then if he wants
to do it in the back of his Lincoln
I think

Fine. Feel young again for all I care.

neesha

I got dis teacha whoz gullectin
color full stewdent dickshun
tho he don beleave me I say the minut
u write sumthin down, its gone
and sumthin better took it splace while
u wasn't lookin.

Butt I toll him da word for 2day
is Swayze.

Iz like "I'm ghost" meanin I yam outta here.
Well Swayze means same thang bee
cause Patrick Swayze was in *Ghost*
with ol Semi-Demi-Moore-please.

Butt I hopi don go chattin up da brotherz
then sayin "I'm Swayze." Dey laff at hiz
white ass butt goode.

Kelli♡

Damon beeped me like twenty times.

Mom's right.

I am too young

to go that steady.

II

CARTER

Hasn't anybody in this town ever seen
a black guy in a cashmere sweater?

Or is it just that they've never seen
a cashmere sweater?

david

Well, video games better be violent, man, because
that's the idea. They let you do something you can't
do in real life!

I don't want to wipe out all the french fry cooks
at McDonald's. I just want to sit down at an
X-Man console and kill a few hundred aliens.

In Japan, the games are way nastier, okay?
And who's got the stratospheric crime rate,
them or us?

Let's say I spend a bunch of money playing Requiem:
The Avenging Angel because Malachi can turn
enemies into salt.

Afterwards, do I want to do that? No way.
It's out of my system.

Boyd

I'm tripping in lit class, thinking about
some of the stuff Mike's been saying when
Ms. Fadiman reads us something about this girl
who quote died unquote.

Then she wants us to free-write about our
idea of heaven. Piece of cake — cheap gas
and a Pontiac Firebird and everybody's white
and no rules and good dope and no parents
UNLESS THEY'LL FUCKING STAY TOGETHER MORE
THAN TEN FUCKING MINUTES and no school
of any kind and big hogass TVs all over plus cool
places to live in nature and shit like that.

When she starts reading again, this chick
is somewhere with angels and a light show
and all of a sudden she hears, "It is not time."

And BAM — she's alive again!!!

"It is not time." Man, that got me. I mean
Mike was just talking about this —
you're invincible until your number comes up.
Fucking invincible.

So why not do it? If it's time, we go out like
warriors. Otherwise, we get to read about
ourselves in the paper.

TRAN

Since I have only acquaintances and no
true friends, I come to school in the morning
and let the building tell me things.

In this way I am like the Native Americans
who could taste water, listen to earth, read
sky.

I listen to what is traveling through wires,
dripping from overhead lighting, radiating
from computer screens, oozing from outlets
in walls:

who lied who kissed who drank who smoked
who struck wept contaminated bought
sold doted barely survived.

This passionate residue is called "the buzz."

What a violent country: "He kissed
me so hard." "I was so wasted." "I hate
her so much." "I love him to death."

The students even call this well-appointed
and modern high school Brimstone,
a reference to their Bible and to the end
of the world.

Jennifer

That troll, Boyd, wrote 666 on his behind
then stood on a chair. Our homeroom teacher,
Ms. Malone, gave him like three years
of detention.

She whispered to me in the hall, "I don't think
we'll be seeing him during the rapture."

She goes to Abundant Life Fellowship with
my folks. And me. Me sometimes. She likes
to talk about Heaven. I'm not sure I'll be
taken up; I have bad thoughts. But if I am,
I wonder if there'll be homework?

I know who won't be there — Neesha
and her friends. Ms. Malone says black
people have their own Heaven, but it's
far enough away from ours so we won't
have to listen to their music.

Kelli

I did it. I gave Damon back

his cell phone

and that damn beeper.

Boyd

I was gonna drop out of school until
Mike got me to see how we need
people who can lead the foot soldiers.
Somebody the grunts can look up to.

So I'll march up there and shake some total
phony's hand.

Plus Mike's springing for a tattoo when I
get my diploma.

joseph

Mom puts everything in the fridge
in the same place every time, so she can
whip open the door, grab what she needs,
and slam it before she wastes one micro
kilowatt of energy.

The rain forest burns at about
ten thousand board feet per minute.
The ozone layer shrinks like a cheap
shirt, and my folks buy gray toilet
paper you could shingle a house with.

Totally out of touch with the real
issues.

One thing I'll never forget, though.
I was little, maybe four years old,
when we went to protest the Nemo Dam.

That first night, all the kids were
in one big tent under a bunch of homemade
quilts. And most of the grownups came
and kissed everybody good night.
And then they sang.

The dam got built anyway, but it's
a sweet memory.

david

Seems like all my parents do
is scream at each other
and every now and then my dad
hurls his dinner at the wall.

I just go upstairs and put on my
headphones or hit the arcade.

I should take Dad, let him work
off some of that aggression.

Gee, if only there was a game called
Flying Spaghetti, he'd be at
the Expert Level first time out.

Allison

I swear to God if my stepfather comes
into my room one more time

I AM GOING TO KILL HIM.

Kelli°

I went to the movies by myself,
saw exactly what I wanted to see,
and stayed all the way through
for once.

I read everybody's name: grip,
best boy, caterer, DG trainee,
everybody.

When I got home Mom said Damon
called

three times.

Lester

I'm about half sick to my stomach all
the time because I'm scared.

Those jocks come down the hall like
a tidal wave of muscle. On a good day
they only knock me into the wall once.

The time Damon smashed a Twinkie
in my face I went to the office and
ratted him out.

I could see Mr. Newman look at his
calendar and think, *The game's tomorrow
night*.

But he said, "I'll talk to him, Lester. We'll
make sure this doesn't happen again."

Next time it was a Ding Dong instead
of a Twinkie. Damon said if I opened
my big mouth, I was a goner.

TRAN

In my religion, we believe in ghosts,
people who cannot go on to paradise,
but cannot be reborn, either.

Hungry ghosts have insatiable appetites
and thirst nothing can satisfy.

Buddhist hungry ghosts are ugly,
with skinny necks and bloated
stomachs.

American ghosts are attractive
but still insatiable: Damon longs
for greater strength, Rob for more
conquests, Neesha for revenge,
Kelli for autonomy. Even Joseph,
who seems so virtuous, craves
recognition.

And me? Haunted by my father's
memories, I am an anthology
of ghosts.

Boyd

Dad makes me go with him to his sister's
house because he wants to borrow some
money.

So he's in the perfect den with perfect
Uncle Wes and I'm out there with Eve's
perfect two-point-five children and she
tells me to take off my boots because
the carpet is new.

Tells me. Doesn't even ask.

Well, fuck that.
So I sit in the car, wrap my coat around
me and smoke. I smoke all the time now
'cause it doesn't matter. "It is not time,"
remember?

And I'm looking at this fucking subdivision
called Clearwater Acres, and there's no
water and no acres, either. Just plots.
Like in a graveyard.

When I exhale and squint, it's like the whole
thing is on fire. All of it — every Plan A,
Plan B, Plan C.

It's beautiful, man. You have no idea.

DAMON

You know what I think'd be great?
A totally athletic high school.
Just all cool guys with good moves,
good hands — the whole package.
You could concentrate early
on a career in the pros.
Get credits for working out.
Screw stuff like history.
My friends and I are already
kings, kings of Branston!

Girls could go to another school.
Then drive over and watch us win.
And afterwards bring us stuff to eat
then dance around in those pants
you can see through.

Kelli

I didn't know
how hard it was
going to be
spending all
this time
alone.

And then I get
to school and
hear Damon like
braying

and I think, *Don't
give up, Kelli.
You can do this.*

meredith

Here's a flash from the frontline:
Older Guys Know How to Kiss.
Most of them, anyway.

The boys around here are pathetic.
I feel like somebody's mining my
mouth with a blunt instrument.
It's like torture. I want to yell,
"I give up. The combination to
the safe is 12-45-75."

But a guy with a wife who doesn't
kiss him anymore except those little
PTA-Doublemint-gum-how-was-your-day
nighty-night pecks,

well, he'll kiss: corner of the mouth,
ripe underlip, light as an angel's
eyelash, wooing kisses: the best.

He knows I'm going all the way
and then some. So he's not kissing
for anything. He's just kissing.
Who could resist a motive so pure?

Boyd

Mike's been cruising the school, hanging out
at Skeeter's, springing for Cokes and chips,
talking the talk.

He wants us to get some more bodies into
the Brotherhood, especially chicks. I said,
"If it's a brotherhood, why do we need
chicks?"

He told me to use my head. Girls can carry shit
in their purses for us.

I asked him if we were like dating these chicks.
And he said no way. Warriors always had like
concubines and harems and stuff.

Girls make me nervous. My dad got all the looks,
all the moves. I'm totally paralyzed around girls.

So I told Mike I'd try to recruit some guys first.
Rob and his crew, maybe. Get like five at one
time.

"Not Rob."
"Why not?"
"He's too fucking good-looking. Put him on
the list."

Lester

I guess it was last Friday this guy
named Boyd, one of those pissed-off
types with paratrooper boots, offered
to kick Damon's ass for me.

I said that'd be great but Damon would
find out and get me twice as bad.

He said no way, and all I had to do was
join some kind of club.

I said I'd think about it.

So today Boyd sat with me at lunch
and now he's talking a mile a minute
about diesel fuel, cotton, newspaper,
and fertilizer.

He says it'll blow up a garage.

I asked what good it'd do to blow up
Damon's garage.

"Who's talking about Damon?"

david

You know what I've been thinking?
That if you go far enough, like all
the way, then you're a hero. But if
you just sort of stay in the middle,
you're a drone.

Take me — I love video games. I'm
good at them. Big scores. Highest
levels.

But my folks are always telling me,
"It's just a game. How are you gonna
make a living? Blah, blah, blah."

I'm halfway through writing the program
for some killer Book of the Dead.
It's gonna be such a cool game! This guy
at school named Tran was telling me all
about Buddhism, which has got like ghosts
and demons and sinister babes and all
kinds of cool stuff.

One wicked game and I'm in the mix.
I see these guys at conventions
with their copycat crap and them
looking all pale and geeky

but they're rich, man. And their parents
are off their backs for good.

Allison

He's doing that back-rub thing
again. And now he's like lurking
in the hall when I come out
of the bathroom.

I might get a gun. The buzz is
Boyd's got some.

I don't even want bullets.
I'm not going to shoot anybody.

But I want to be sitting at my computer
when he starts being "friendly." I'll
have the gun in my lap and I'll just
pick it up and turn around and point
it right at his crotch and not even say
one word.

CARTER

Here's the demographic breakdown
when it comes to whom I remind people
of: anybody in their fifties, I'm Sidney
Poitier; if they're in their thirties,
I'm Denzel Washington; and it's Will
Smith to everybody else including
the local Kelli who's probably just talking
to me to make her jock boyfriend jealous.

We're only here for a little while so my dad
can learn some techniques from this other
surgeon in the city.

Which is what he wants me to be even though
I can hear a song once, then sit down at the piano
and play it. *And sometimes make it better.*

But I'm supposed to be a doctor, too. Forget
what I'm good at, what I really like to do.
Just so we're the Sanford & Son of medicine.

Kelli

I like Damon
more when I don't see
him so much.

So if I didn't see him
at all, would I
love him?

DAMON

It amazes me what I can do. Twenty
sets of twenty? No sweat. A thousand
crunches? Fine. Four miles? You got it.

Sure, I get tired. But next day I'm fine.
Stronger than ever.

Some candyass in English works on
his little sonnet, okay? Cuts this,
adds that.

That's what I do in the gym! Take some
fat away here, put some muscle there.
Until I'm perfect.

Now I'm a poem, faggot.

III

Boyd

We make plans, we download from that
supersecret website, we draw diagrams,
or go on a weapons recon, and Mike just
gets calmer.

Not me. I keep both fists in my pockets
and nod. Otherwise my voice, my hands,
everything shakes.

Then I look at the list: everybody who
ever blew me off, flipped me off,
or pissed me off.

So I shake a little. It'll be worth it.

david

My parents got on my case again
and I went off on them.

They said I never used to be like
that until I got addicted to violence.

I AM NOT ADDICTED TO VIOLENCE.
I just like to play video games.
There's a big goddamned difference.

Maybe I'll shelve that Book of the Dead
and start writing a game
called Guts on the Good Rug.

joseph

Let's say I kill somebody, but I use
a silk scarf that matches their
outfit. Does that make it okay?

That's what the land rapers do when
they claim their dam will "fit into
the environment." They strangle
the river with a big silk scarf.

Major protest a hundred miles from
here on the banks of the Little Nero.

My parents can stay home, write
letters, and visualize world peace.

I'm going.

kitty

I think if I'm thin enough, I can fly.

I'll get real thin and just levitate.
Lift off.

I like the way birds leave home.
They just go.

Nobody's crying, nobody's lecturing.

I read about these birds that almost
never land:

they feed on the wing, nap as they
glide, never make a nest.

They weigh next to nothing.

joseph

A big guy in overalls gave a little speech
before the bulldozers showed up. He talked
about this concept called Satyagraha.

It's to make the cops work: you just go
limp and they have to carry you away.

And the fatter you are, the better you'd
be at Satyagraha. All the pale vegans
in their Birkenstocks get hauled away
like so many weeds.

Where are the big mommas and poppas
who love the earth, a cop on each limb,
all four of 'em sweating bullets?

Where's Lester when I need him?

ROB

Everybody in my posse says
Jennifer can't be had.

I say she can.

david

Octogon peed his pants when he saw Ninja
in Metal Gear Solid, okay?

I know how he feels. I'm like 5'4" and I want
to pee mine just about every day walking
into high school. I saw Damon come down
so hard on Lester the other day I couldn't
believe it.

Lester

I'm going to hook up with Boyd, after all.
I need some friends, man. Somebody to
watch my back.

Damon blind-sided me again after school.
I went down hard. Skinned my arm and
everything while his buddies and their
airhead girlfriends laughed.

Boyd says there's an initiation and I'll
have to buy some different clothes.

Okay, fine. So I'll be an anarchist.
I'm nothing now but a fat kid.

Boyd

Mike and I welcomed Lester to the Brotherhood.
We beat on him pretty good, and he took it.
Then we got out the tequila.

Now we're bonded. I'll do my part, too.
I'll keep Damon off Lester's ass.

Then when the time comes, he'll hump
the stuff into school in his backpack.

Last night reminded me of my initiation.
Just Mike and me in his garage. He fucking
broke a rib and I didn't even grunt.

Went to the school nurse the next day
just to make sure it didn't puncture a lung.

She wanted to know who did it.

"Bunch of black guys jumped me."
"Go to the police."
"Nah, I'll handle it myself."

She liked that. She taped me up really good.
On the way out she said, "If those are the same
hoodlums that ripped off my VCR, give 'em
one for me."

CARTER

There's this Vietnamese guy who never
raises his hand in class but almost always
knows the answer.

Mr. Maxwell calls on everybody else first,
even Boyd, who's usually drawing another
swastika on his arm with a Pilot pen.

Then he looks at Tran or me.

Turns out he's a musician too. Plays
this anorexic banjo called a dan tin.

We jammed over at his place the other
day, which is an apartment above his
parents' store. He gave me a sanh sua,
this little percussion thing. So I made
cricket sounds while he wailed on
the dan tin.

It was great. Then he taught me what
he says is the only Vietnamese word
I need to know: *xin*, pronounced like
seen. It means cool.

Xin Tran. Or maybe Tran xin.

Boyd

That gook Train or Tran or whatever
his name is goes on the list.

Fucker answers every question,
won't give anybody else
a chance.

Sheila

I'm totally in love with Monica.
I think about her all the time.

I went to this special bookstore
in the city and bought this guide:
places for girls to stay.

There are these like communes —
no meat, no dairy, no guys.

Anybody can live there if she works
hard and follows the rules.

I want to go farther with Monica
than just good-bye hugs.

She makes my knees weak.

I'm waiting for a good time
to show her the book. Tell her
about my plans.

Lester

So I'm in.
And I've got a split lip to show for it.

And all I could do was stand there and take
it. That was the rule. Hands at my sides.

The funny thing is I liked not being able
to fight back.

With Damon and those guys, I won't.
I guess I'm a coward.

With Mike and Boyd, I couldn't.
I was following orders.

One way I'm chickenshit. The other
a good soldier.

Then we all got drunk.

This morning Meredith said she liked
my new look.

When's the last time a girl talked to me first?
Amazing!

joseph

RAPACIOUS. What a great word. It
describes man to a T, doesn't it?

Man, the Great Imbalancer. Land raper,
river raper, cloud raper.

Take, grab, hoard, spend, rip, seize,
pillage, ransack, plunder, spoil,
defile, abuse, violate.

What swine we are. And proud
of it in our belching cars and fat
guts. Proud swine.

Man, I try to talk to people and they
make fun of me, just like they do
Jennifer's dad standing outside
school with a handful of tracts.

He believes in a better world
after this one. I know this is the only
world we've got, and we're treating
it like shit!

IV

DAMON

I twisted my ankle. Again. And Coach
told me to be *really* careful. I already
had arthro on both knees.

Sometimes I catch these old jocks
on TV doing color and interviews
and I swear to God I can see it
in their eyes, how they miss the game.

I could hold the microphone, I guess.
Kelli's good at speech, so she could
give me some pointers.

Except she's not talking to me since
she got like nonstop PMS or something.

I told her when we get to State,
she's going to have to shape up.

Kelli

I've got good grades and my folks
can afford to send me anyplace.

Damon can yell all he wants.

I can yell too. I didn't think
I could. But I can.

I AM NOT GOING TO STATE.

Jennifer

Reverend Powell said the Antichrist
is not a beast with horns and a tail,
but someone beautiful and charismatic.

I thought it was Marilyn Manson.

Rob is the best-looking boy in school.
I know he's awful but in class the other
day the teacher made him read a poem.

Rob's voice was beautiful — deep and rich.
And he was wearing the cutest shirt.

I didn't want to listen to him or look at him,
but I couldn't help myself.

neesha

Your mind strikes out
While your lower lip pouts
You think you're a smart one
With your purple Doc Martens
But you don't have no clout.

You stomp around the school
Thinkin you're cool
You never do your lessons
Except your Nazi rantin sessions
Snowin nobody, you poor fool.

You're dissin left and right
Dissin everything in sight
Snotty little bitch
Back-stabbin little snitch
Better get ready for a fight.

Black is beautiful
Black is fruitful
Black is sorrowful
Black is powerful.

I stand by my sisters and brothers
All the rest are punk-ass mothers.

Boyd

In speech class yesterday, Neesha stands up and raps out this piece, glaring at me the whole time.

I sat there thinking that she's inferior and all but I respect how she stands up for herself.

But it was a mistake to call me a bitch.

CARTER

I'm strolling past the Dark Town table
the other day when this Neesha who laid
into Boyd in class starts carrying on
about the history of rap.

She's throwing names around (Mad
Cobra, Captain Quad, 40-B-Low)
and she knows her stuff, too.

And then she asks this rhetorical
question, one she doesn't think there's
an answer to because she has covered
the territory so the audience is snowed
by her erudition.

"Anybody," she says all cockylike,
"that I forgot?"

And I'm the last person — me with my
meat loaf and peas and my Ralph Lauren
polo — she expects to hear from.

"How about Shango?" I say. "Remember
Afrika Bambaataa and Soul Sonic Force?"

She flashes me a look that could've melted
my Jell-O. "That's right. Thank you, my
brother."

She's trouble, I tell myself. *Self — are you
listening?*

david

Boyd cornered me in gym yesterday.
Wants me to join some kind
of brotherhood. Tried three times
to pronounce *apocalypse*, then gave up
and said something bad was going
to happen and which side did I want
to be on?

Now there's a guy that never played
a minute of Doom or Quake or
Donkey Kong as far as I know

and just look at him!

Rob

I told Jennifer what she wanted
to hear.

It was so easy I'm kind of ashamed
to get double points for her.

Jennifer

Rob is so cute. If he picks me up
at my girlfriend's house, Dad
won't ask him if he knows Jesus.

Boyd

I was telling Lester about pipe bombs.
He said, "The kind you smoke?"

Cracked me up. Mike's right. Lester's
expendable. He goes in first.

Mike says we need passports 'cause
we're almost outlaws already. He said
the FBI's for sure flagged our website.

If they come for us, we're gone. Mike
says he's got friends everywhere. We'll
just disappear. The big Swayze.

He said to maybe tell my dad good-bye
real casual-like sometime.

Yeah? And where exactly would I find him?

Jennifer

On television when couples get on the bed
the camera goes over to a painting of the ocean
or something.

There was one of those at the Holiday Inn, so
I looked at it while Rob took off his clothes.

I wanted to keep my bra on and he said that
was okay.

It was kind of gross him lying on me like that,
plus it hurt.

I should have told him to stop but I didn't.

The only part I liked was when he kissed me.

Oh, man. I showed Monica that commune thing
and *she just freaked.*

Told me no way. Told me to just forget it.
Told me to quit bothering her!

She said, "I'm not like you. I'm no dyke!"

I'm no dyke, either. I'm just in love
with Monica.

joseph

People split because there were only
chemical toilets. Because it got cold
and rained. Because they couldn't hook up
with some super-earnest chick with hair
under her arms.

The ones who did stay spent one night in jail
and felt like saints. Then they went home
and surfed the Net looking for the next road
to sit in and sing "We Shall Overcome."

You know what nonviolent means: *nothing
ever changes.*

Jennifer

Boyd stopped me after gym and said he'd
take care of Rob for me.

"What?"

"He raped you, didn't he?"

"I don't know."

"So do you want him on the list or not?"

What would Jesus do?

CARTER

Tran says he's on Boyd's list.
I'm there, too. And Neesha.

I can't take Boyd seriously. He looks
like he's all dressed up for the
Anarchists' Dance.

It's still kind of ironic: my folks
thought coming here would be better,
safer. That's why Dad drives forty-five
minutes to the hospital.

Well, in D.C. I was a black guy with money,
which made me almost white.

Here I'm just a black guy.

Or worse.

Boyd

We're driving back
from State Line Guns & Ammo
one last time.

Mike's got a joint in one hand,
a beer in the other, we're
going about a hundred miles
an hour and he's yelling over
the tape deck about next week:
pistols in every pocket, bombs
in the backpacks, rifles under
the coats.

I've been blazin' it, too, so
I'm pounding on the dashboard
and howlin' out the window,
except every now and then I get
this little like twinge and I want
to tell Mike to just slow down.

And then I think: too late now,
man. We couldn't stop if we
wanted to.

Lester

I'm in the cafeteria the other day
and I'm thinking how tired I am of eating
by myself.

Kitty's more pathetic than I am. At least
I eat what I buy. Joseph with his beard looks
like one of those bushes he's trying to save
from evil land developers. Sheila is crying
about her girlfriend who's all over Damon.

I figure, *What the hell. Sit with Meredith.*

Turns out she is really pretty nice. I mean,
she's smart and funny and she talked to me
like I was worth talking to.

I know her reputation, but what about Rob?
He keeps score and he's called a stud.

Meredith sleeps with a few guys and she's
a slut.

Anybody called her that while I was around,
I wouldn't even tell Boyd. I'd put the hurt
on him myself.

Sheila

I saw Monica with Damon.
Again.

Oh, God. I just want to
kill myself.

V

joseph

I'm fed up with Gandhi and Martin Luther
King. Sometimes you've got to get people's
attention!

So I go over to Boyd's house.

He's pretty ragged. "Hey, man. You just
missed Sheila." Then he opens up this old cedar
chest and shows me.

"I got a Ruger and I got a Smith & Wesson."
Then he picks up this Glock, holds it. "First
time Mike gave me one of these, I almost
puked."

When I ask him if he's okay, he reaches
into his camouflage pants and shows me
a handful of pills. "Yeah, until I forget
which of these do what." Then he hands
me the Ruger. "Try this one. See if it
feels good."

No way. I've got my hands up like he's
an ATM robber. "Look, you haven't been
at school. I was worried." He shrugs.
"Whatever." Walks me to the door. Hugs me.
Says to miss first period on Tuesday.

Out in the car, I just sit there. Is he serious?
I mean, I've heard stuff, but I always hear stuff:
it's high school, right? And anyway, who would
I tell, the same cops who dragged me to jail
the time I handcuffed myself to that bulldozer?

And then I start thinking: So he's got a couple
of guns. He used to have a lot of skin
magazines. That didn't make him a rapist.
And last summer, who came and got me
in the rain when I blew a tire way the hell
out on Maxwell Road in the middle
of the night?

Boyd, that's who.

Lester

Meredith and I went out last night.
A milestone for me — a real date!

Well, okay, she met me at Skeeter's,
but still . . .

She's going to go to college. I was totally
surprised. She busted me on it, too:
"What'd you think? That a girl like me
is always stupid?"

I finally said, "I guess so. I'm sorry."
Then she leaned across the table and kissed
me. On the cheek, but a kiss is a kiss.

"That's for being honest with me. There
aren't that many honest guys around."

I walked her home, which is this apartment
building that looks like Alcatraz.

"Lester, what's this list I keep hearing about?"

"Just people that Mike and Boyd hate."

"They've got a lot of guns, right?"

"I guess. They don't talk to me much
anymore."

"Stay away from those guys, Lester."

"But Boyd keeps Damon off my case."

"It's not worth it, honey. Promise me you'll
stay away.

Honey. Oh, man I liked the sound of that.

Boyd

Mike drew a big red circle around
the 17th, just like Mom used to
for my birthday.

TRAN

Carter and I play music together
two nights a week. Through him I
know Neesha, who is not as forbidding
as she appears.

David, also, is a good person.
He likes to hear about the journey
after death. He introduced me
to video games. He is very adept.

These people are my friends.
Nothing should happen to them
because of my cowardice or
indecision.

meredith

Boyd runs into me today. Says he
needs a favor. Will I do his buddy,
Mike, that guy with the bad teeth
who works down at the ARCO station.

I said, "No way."

He says, "What's one more?"

I thought I was drowning; my life
sort of flashed in front of my eyes.
Guys slobbering on me, guys whose
names I can't even remember.

And then Boyd's pissed. "You're on
the list now," he said. "You'll be sorry."

I told him, "I'm already sorry."

TRAN

When I called the police, someone said,
"And you are?"

I spelled my name many times.

"So what can I do for you?"

When I told him he asked, "Have you
seen these guns?"

I said, "No, but . . ."

"So how do you know? Somebody tell
you?"

The wires, the overhead lights, the
computer screens, the outlets in
the walls.

"I just know."

"This guy Boyd, you haven't got some
kind of beef with him, have you?"

"No."

"So this isn't just an easy way to get
him in trouble."

"I assure you, it is not."

"You assure me, huh? Okay,
we'll look into it."

Lester

After Boyd yelled at me, I went right over
to Meredith's and told her everything.

She said the coolest thing: "Boyd wants you
to stop him."

"Are you kidding? He called me a traitor.
He said I'm on that list now."

"He doesn't know he wants you to stop
him, but he does."

I asked her, "What if I rat him out and Mike's
moved the stash or something? Then I'm
really in trouble."

She said, "What if you don't and he starts
shooting people?"

I told her I was scared. She said, "And I'm not?
Look, we'll go to the cops together, okay?"

I'm probably in love with her, whatever
that means.

And if this backfires and Boyd so much as
looks at her funny afterwards, I'll kill him.

CARTER

I'm not black enough for her friends,
she's too black for my mom. "Two
households both alike in dignity,"
now that I think about it. Shakespeare
in the hood.

I don't know what to do about this.
We really like each other. She says
she can relax around me, doesn't have
to be Foxy Brown twenty-four seven.

And I like being around somebody
who's never heard of Jack & Jill,
Fortune 500, or black cotillions.

She hangs around Tran's place while
he and I work on chord progressions.
I like to look up and see her there.
She usually sleeps because it's
noisy where she lives.

Lately she just sits by the window.
I ask her, "Wassup?"

"Boyd's out there somewhere."

"So?"

"So I'm watchin' your back.
You go on and play the piano.
Leave Boyd to me."

neesha

Carter's a sweet boy. Thas how I think
of him, u no? Innocent. He always walkin
around like he belong here, like this is
Eden before the big apple scandal.

Only time Carter seen a brother lyin in
the street that be the Triple A man
fixin his mamma's Mercedes.

My crew they don't want much to dew
wif Carter. They call him the Oreoist
Oreo they ever seen.

Maybe, but they pretty much all show
and no go. Everything be tomorrow
for sure. Pretty soon. Next time.

Carter — he do it now: make all A's,
play piano like nobody's business, take
up with this Tran dude and make some
I mean strange music.

Good thing I don't love him. His leaving
brake my entire heart.

Boyd

It's tomorrow.

Lester

At first, the cops wouldn't believe me.
I'd tell one of 'em the whole story and he'd
pick up his phone. Then another one would
come out and I'd tell him, and he'd stare
at me and then disappear.

That's when Meredith loses it. "If you dumb
shits want to be the next ones talking to Larry
King and trying to explain why you didn't
prevent another tragedy, that's fine with us."
And she grabs my arm and starts toward the door.

Finally a guy fatter than me
says, "Hold on. I just remembered this call from
some Chinese kid."

What they did was take us along and make us
sit in the back of the black-and-white while
one of them goes up to the house and the other
one like frowns at us over the seat.

I'm telling you, I was holding Meredith's hand
so tight it probably hurt.

Then Boyd's dad opens the front door. The cop
takes off his hat, says something, and in he goes.

Five minutes later he comes out. He's jogging
this time and he's totally pale, a ghost cop,
and he leans in and says, "There's a goddamned
arsenal in there. Call for backup, and call
the bomb squad."

I relax for the first time in, I don't know, weeks.
I close my eyes, put my arm around Meredith.

Pretty soon there's all kinds of sirens,
cops with yellow tape and those stripey
barriers, some kind of armored car with
SWAT on the side, and Boyd's dad running
up and down the block probably telling
anybody who'll listen he thought his
kid was doing homework down there.

We just sit tight and listen to the crackly
police radio: the bomb squad guys go in
first.

Meredith sits up, listens, looks out the window.
"The Channel 7 chopper. You're gonna be on
the news."

And without even thinking about it, I say, "Oh,
man. TV makes you look fatter." And Meredith
starts laughing. Then I start and we can't stop.
It's not that funny, but we're like so relieved
that we're falling all over each other. Then
her nose starts running, so that's funny and
the only thing that stops us is when they
bring Boyd out all handcuffed with even
his ankles chained together like he's Hannibal
Lecter or something.

They're going to put him in the car behind
the one we're in, so he gets a glimpse
of me through the window. And you know
what he says?

"Hey, Lester."

That's it. Not traitor, not scumbag, not
chicken shit. Just, "Hey, Lester."

VI

kitty

Thank God

it didn't
happen.

If I got shot
and had to go
to the hospital

they'd make me

eat.

DAMON

I knew that'd never go down.
Boyd's always been nothing
but a bigmouthed punk.

And who'd believe that Lester
would ever blow up the
cafeteria!

You know, I'll bet all this is what
upset Kelli. She hates violence.

Plus she's gotta be jealous 'cause
Monica can't keep her hands off me.

I'll bet she'll want her beeper
back tomorrow.

Sheila

I handed my mom the gun I bought from Boyd.
The first thing she did was cry. She said
I had to give it to the cops and tell them
where I got it. Then I had to talk to
a shrink.

I start to cry and tell her about Monica.

She just gets her keys and points us toward
the police station. I think I know what's
coming next: what kind of daughter she raised,
how much trouble I am, where's the money
for therapy going to come from.

Instead she told me when she was my age
she had a crush on some girl, too.

I stared at her. She just shrugged.

"I wasn't always a mom."

joseph

What was I doing over
at Boyd's the other night?
Who was I gonna be, Smokey
Bear with a piece?

I feel real stupid about
that and about not telling
the cops. I'm glad Lester
came through.

One thing I don't feel stupid
about is waiting so long
to ask Jennifer to the prom.

Now I don't want to. Not
after what happened with Rob.

I mean, everybody knows
what Rob's like. So why
did she go out with him?

Allison

After it was all over, people freaked
out, even though nothing happened.

So they brought these counselors in.
I found this lady who looked nice

and told her I wanted one of Boyd's
guns once because of what my stepdad

was doing. She looked at me over her
glasses. "Go on." When I did, she said,

"Oh, honey." And then she wrote down
everything I said.

Lester

I was a hero for about ten minutes.
Then teachers started asking me for
my homework.

Damon gave me a ration of shit because
I ratted out Boyd.

I stood my ground, looked him straight
in the eye, held my fists like Mike showed
me, and told him I was going right for his
knees.

He thought that one over.

More good news — Meredith and I are going
to the prom. So I really am going to lose
some weight, like ten pounds at least.
I sure don't want to rent the biggest
tux in the world.

Rob

Man, I was on that list.
I don't get it?

What'd I do?

Jennifer

Where was God that night at the Holiday
Inn?

And where's Joseph now?

I know he was going to ask me
to the prom. I know it!

meredith

Lester is so sweet. Sometimes we sit
for hours and don't say ten words.

He's the only boy I ever knew who'll
just hold me.

Oh, sure, he wants more. He's eighteen.
But I can't right now.

I figure college is a good place to
just start over.

Lester knows I'm going and he's not.
We just don't talk about it.

CARTER

I sit at Neesha's table in the cafeteria now.
Some of her friends are okay once you get
they're all half Puff Daddy and half
Michael Jordan.

She says that's okay, says I'm half Wynton
Marsalis, half Dr. Kildare.

We're together all the time. My folks just
let it alone. They know a few weeks
and we're ghost.

We're Swayze.

We're gone.

Lester

Mike disappeared. Boyd's eighteen,
so he's really in trouble.

Right up till graduation I hung with
David and Tran. Carter told me
thanks for probably saving his life.
That was cool.

Tran's going to Stanford. He's thin,
so I tried to eat what he did,
but I was hungry all the time.

David's already at community college
taking art and computer classes.
He says next semester I should just
sign up for general ed stuff till I
figure out what I want to do.

He says there's girls all over the place.

Maybe.

I mean, Meredith liked me. Somebody
else might too.

Ron Koertge is the author of several acclaimed novels, including *Where the Kissing Never Stops*, *The Arizona Kid*, and *Tiger, Tiger, Burning Bright*, all of which were ALA Best Books for Young Adults. Of *The Brimstone Journals*, he says, "Usually, I choose characters and settings that are humorous and offbeat. *The Brimstone Journals*, however, chose me. I began the book before the tragedy in Colorado, and the characters woke me up at night. The entire first draft took just three weeks. Then the voices were gone and it was time to be a writer again instead of merely taking dictation from god-knows-where." Ron Koertge lives in South Pasadena, California.